THE TROUBLE WITH TIME TRAVEL

WRITTEN BY
STEPHEN W. MARTIN

ILLUSTRATED BY
CORNELIA LI

OWLKIDS BOOKS

CRASH!

Max and Boomer were in trouble.
Big trouble.

·MAXENE·

The vase was a family heirloom that had originally belonged to Max's great-great-great-great-great-great-grandma.

It was the only thing she had managed to save when her houseboat mysteriously sank in 1785.

How could Max fix this? She had
to think fast. Thankfully, that's
what she did best.

Then it hit her. She could
come clean, or …

… she could build a
TIME MACHINE!

Surprisingly, it was **pretty easy**.

The plan was simple. All she had to do was travel
to the past and smash her great-great-great-
great-great-great-grandma's vase.
Then there would be nothing for
her to break in the future.

Brilliant!

Hopefully, it would work.
The risks were huge. They could
completely tangle the string of time.

Or worse, Max and Boomer could end
up stuck somewhere … **forever.**

Still, she had no choice.
She had to try!

KABOOOOOM!

Max immediately regretted her decision.

Boomer
not so much.

Traveling through time was extremely difficult.
Everywhere Max and her dog went—

past,

future,

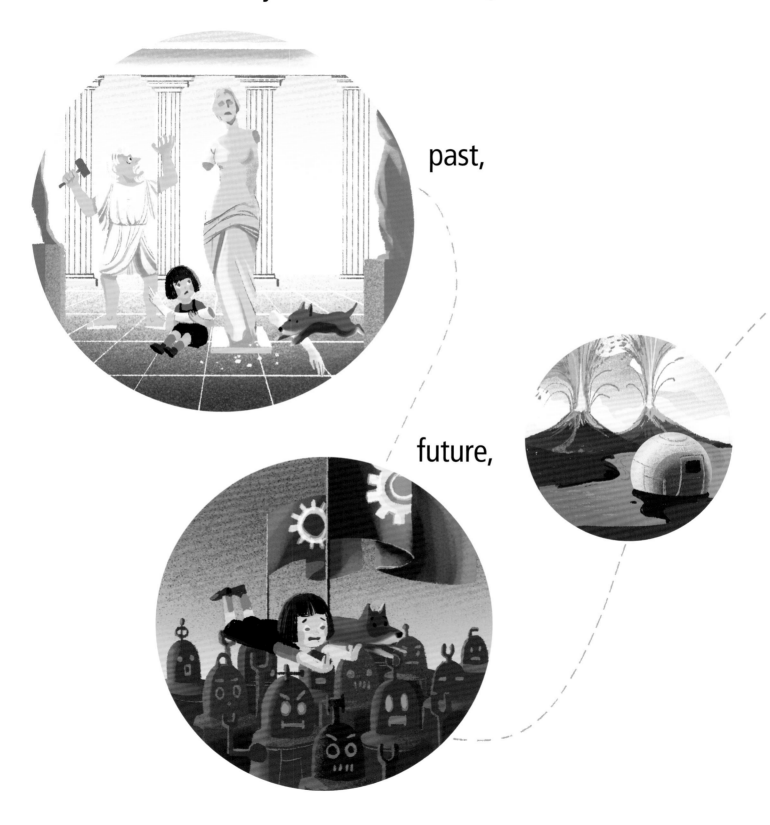

or **whenever** this was—

something went wrong!

And then …

well, this happened …

Max's great-great-great-great-great-great-grandma was not pleased.

Max knew in her heart it was time to give up.

"I never should have built the time machine!" she thought.

"If I had just come clean in the beginning, none of this would have happened!"

That's when it hit her.

She knew what she had to do!

It took a few tries, but they had
a lot of time to get it right.

"Whatever you do," Max said to Max, "do not build a time machine!"

"I can build a time machine?" asked Max.

"Yes, it's surprisingly easy, but DON'T BUILD IT!" said Max as she and Boomer hopped back into their time machine.

"That was strange," thought Max, as she watched herself disappear into a ball of lightning and smoke. "Oh well."

Max picked up Boomer's Frisbee and tossed it with all her might. **"Fetch!"**

For my beautiful wife, Lola—the future leader of the
human resistance and scourge of the machines.

—S.M.

To my mom, who allowed the bedroom walls
to be my first canvas.

—C.L.

Text © 2019 Stephen W. Martin | Illustrations © 2019 Cornelia Li

Owlkids Books acknowledges the financial support of the Canada Council for the Arts,
the Ontario Arts Council, the Government of Canada through the Canada Book Fund (CBF)
and the Government of Ontario through the Ontario Creates Book Initiative
for our publishing activities.

Published in Canada by Owlkids Books Inc., 1 Eglinton Avenue East, Toronto, ON M4P 3A1
Published in the US by Owlkids Books Inc., 1700 Fourth Street, Berkeley, CA 94710

Library of Congress Control Number: 2018963955

Library and Archives Canada Cataloguing in Publication

Title: The trouble with time travel / written by Stephen W. Martin ; illustrated by Cornelia Li.

Names: Martin, Stephen W., 1981- author. | Li, Cornelia, illustrator.

Identifiers: Canadiana 20189065133 | ISBN 9781771473323 (hardcover)

Classification: LCC PS8626 A77294 T75 2019 | DDC jC813/.6—dc23

Edited by Sarah Howden | Designed by Alisa Baldwin

Manufactured in Shenzhen, Guangdong, China, in April 2019, by C & C Offset
Job #HT2087

A   B   C   D   E   F

ONTARIO ARTS COUNCIL
CONSEIL DES ARTS DE L'ONTARIO
an Ontario government agency
un organisme du gouvernement de l'Ontario

Canada Council   Conseil des Arts
for the Arts   du Canada

Canada

Publisher of Chirp, Chickadee and OWL   Owlkids Books is a division of   bayard canada
www.owlkidsbooks.com